For Jerry – J.D.

For Dartington Playgroup – N.S.

First published 2012 by Macmillan Children's Books

This edition published 2013 by Macmillan Children's Books

a division of Macmillan Publishers Limited

20 New Wharf Road, London N1 9RR

Basingstoke and Oxford

Associated companies throughout the world

www.panmacmillan.com

ISBN: 978-1-4472-1094-8

Text copyright © Julia Donaldson 2012

Illustrations copyright © Nick Sharratt 2012

1 3 5 7 9 8 6 4 2

A CIP catalogue record for this book is available from the British Library.

Printed in China

Written by
Julia Donaldson

Illustrated by
Nick Sharratt

Goat Goes To Playgroup

MACMILLAN CHILDREN'S BOOKS

Playgroup has begun.

Time to have some fun.

Cat hangs up her coat.

Don't be silly, Goat!

Squirrel likes the sand.

Goat has joined a band.

A pot of paint for Weasel.

Goat knocks down an easel.

Dog puts on a dress.

Goat is in a mess.

A bunch of grapes for Goose.

Goat has spilt his juice.

Monkey has a cuddle.

Goat is in a puddle.

Mouse is sowing seeds.

Goat pulls up the weeds.

Squirrel likes to sing.

Goat falls off the swing.

Badger reads a book.

Goat decides to cook.

Now it's circle time.

Goat would rather climb.

Home time – look who's come!

Can you see Goat's mum?